D0365772

BESS'S
LOG CABIN
QUILT

OTHER YEARLING BOOKS YOU WILL ENJOY:

NEKOMAH CREEK, *Linda Crew*
NEKOMAH CREEK CHRISTMAS, *Linda Crew*
CALICO BUSH, *Rachel Field*
HITTY: HER FIRST HUNDRED YEARS, *Rachel Field*
THIMBLE SUMMER, *Elizabeth Enright*
I AM REGINA, *Sally M. Keehn*
CALICO CAPTIVE, *Elizabeth George Speare*
THE WITCH OF BLACKBIRD POND, *Elizabeth George Speare*
THE IRON DRAGON NEVER SLEEPS, *Stephen Krensky*
MR. TUCKET, *Gary Paulsen*

YEARLING BOOKS are designed especially to entertain and enlighten young people. Patricia Reilly Giff, consultant to this series, received her bachelor's degree from Marymount College and a master's degree in history from St. John's University. She holds a Professional Diploma in Reading and a Doctorate of Humane Letters from Hofstra University. She was a teacher and reading consultant for many years, and is the author of numerous books for young readers.

For a complete listing of all Yearling titles, write to
Dell Readers Service,
P.O. Box 1045,
South Holland, IL 60473.

BESS'S
LOG CABIN
QUILT

D. Anne Love

drawings by Ronald Himler

A Yearling Book

For Ron, with all my love
D.A.L.

Published by
Bantam Doubleday Dell Books for Young Readers
a division of
Bantam Doubleday Dell Publishing Group, Inc.
1540 Broadway
New York, New York 10036

If you purchased this book without a cover you should be aware that this book is stolen property. It was reported as "unsold and destroyed" to the publisher and neither the author nor the publisher has received any payment for this "stripped book."

Text copyright © 1995 by D. Anne Love
Illustrations copyright © 1995 by Holiday House, Inc.

All rights reserved. No part of this book may be reproduced or transmitted in any form or by any means, electronic or mechanical, including photocopying, recording, or by any information storage and retrieval system, without the written permission of the Publisher, except where permitted by law. For information address Holiday House, Inc., New York, New York 10017.

The trademarks Yearling® and Dell® are registered in the U.S. Patent and Trademark Office and in other countries.

ISBN: 0-440-41197-1

Reprinted by arrangement with Holiday House

Printed in the United States of America

November 1996

10 9 8 7 6 5 4 3 2 1

CWO

Chapter One

"Ouch!" Bess dropped her silver needle and sucked on her finger, scowling. "I *hate* quilting, Mama! The needle sticks and the threads get all knotted."

Mama looked up from her own work, her gray eyes merry. "You're always in such a hurry, dear. To make a fine quilt, you must have patience. Here, let me see your finger."

Bess held out her hand. Mama studied it and said, "No harm done. The skin's not even broken."

Then she kissed each of Bess's fingers, making loud smacking sounds until Bess giggled out loud. Mama could make anything fun. Even something so tiresome as working on a quilt.

Through the open doorway, Bess could see the patch of soft summer grass that sloped away from their cabin and down to the river. A meadowlark sang from the top of the fir trees and a warm breeze stirred the flowers Mama planted beside the gate. Bess sighed. It was much too fine a day to waste working on an old quilt.

"Mama, may I go now?" Bess asked. "It'll be dark soon and I still have my chores to do."

Mama smiled. "And just when did you become so interested in milking cows and feeding chickens?"

She handed Bess her quilting needle. "Just a few more rows and then we'll stop for today, I promise."

Bess tried to make her needle move smoothly up and down through the strips of cloth like Mama's did. But no matter how she tried, the thread always wound up in an ugly lump. She sighed so loudly that Mama looked up from her quilting and said, "Come on, Bess, it can't be as bad as all that. Is something else bothering you?"

"I miss Papa," Bess said. Sudden tears rolled down her cheeks. "He should have been back weeks ago."

Mama's hands stilled and her expression grew serious. "I miss him, too, darling. But he'll be back any day now. And just think of all the wonderful stories he'll have to tell."

Bess brushed away her tears. "I love Papa's stories."

"Me too," Mama said. "And after seven months with the wagon train, he'll have hundreds of them."

"Will there be anyone my age on the train this time?" Bess asked.

"I shouldn't be at all surprised," Mama said. "Surely out of three hundred new settlers there will be one ten-year-old in the bunch."

"I hope it's a girl," Bess said. "But I'm so lonesome right now, I wouldn't even care if it was a boy. As long as he was nice."

Mama picked up her needle again. It went in and out along the strips of brown and red and blue and yellow cloth, making perfect stitches so small Bess had to squint to see them.

"Poor Bess," she said softly. "Oregon

is a lonely place for a young girl. When you're old enough, Papa and I will send you to a fine school in the East. You'll have plenty of friends for company then."

"Oh, I'm *never* leaving you and Papa," Bess declared. "Not even when I'm a hundred years old. I'd miss you too much, Mama. And I'd miss Papa's stories, and his music."

"That's what's missing around here," Mama said. "Music!"

She got to her feet and the quilt slid to the floor. She grabbed Bess's hands and twirled her around the cabin, humming "Turkey in the Straw." Round and round the cabin they twirled until Bess felt dizzy and weak with laughter. Mama laughed too, and her smooth brown braids came undone and flapped around her head when she danced.

"Faster, Mama, faster!" Bess cried,

and they twirled some more, their shoes scraping and thumping on the wooden floor. Then, Mama suddenly stopped dancing and slumped to the floor.

Bess knelt beside her. "Mama? Are you all right?"

Mama's eyes looked clouded. Little beads of sweat stood on her forehead. "I'll be all right. Just let me rest here a minute."

Bess ran to the porch and filled the dipper with cool water. "Here, Mama, drink this," she said, holding the dipper to her mother's lips.

Mama sipped the water and closed her eyes. "Too much dancing," she muttered. "Guess I'm too old for such foolishness. Help me up, Bess."

Bess put her arm around her mother's waist and helped her to the feather bed in the corner. She drew up the covers and put another glass of water beside the bed.

"Thank you, Bess," her mother said. "You go on and do your chores now. It's way past milking time. Old Sybil will be looking for you."

"Will you be all right?" Bess asked.

"I'll be fine. When you come back we'll make flapjacks for supper. Go on now."

Bess kissed her mother's cheek and took the milk pail from its nail on the porch. She unlatched the gate and went to find Sybil. Between the cabin and the pasture was the new orchard Papa had planted as soon as the Morgan family arrived in Oregon. The fruit trees were no fatter than Bess's finger, and came barely up to her knees, but someday, they would grow strong, and taller than the roof of their cabin. Then there would be pears and cherries to sell at the market in Salem.

Bess stopped to check on the onion

patch. It was late summer, and most of the onions were already harvested. She and Mama had pulled them from the black earth and put them in netting to dry. When winter came, they would have plenty of sweet onions for roasting and soup making.

The afternoon sun slanted through the tall trees beside the river. Bess watched the sunlight dancing on the water and thought of home. Back in Missouri, her friends would be playing in the murky swimming hole on Jimmy Bartlett's farm. Ellen and Mary and Caroline would be planning what to wear to the church social on Sunday, and Freddie Smith and his brothers would be out on the water in their leaky old rowboat, fishing for catfish.

Bess swallowed a big lump in her throat. Why couldn't Papa have been happy in Missouri? He was the editor of

8

the town newspaper, the *Tribune,* and everyone loved him. They had a fine white house on a street lined with tall trees. Roses grew in the yard and along their fence. Bess had her very own tree house, and dresses made of satin and lace, so unlike the plain brown cotton ones she wore now.

But Papa had caught something. Something the newspaper called Oregon Fever. Kit Carson and Jim Bridger told wonderful stories about Oregon. It was a beautiful land, they said, a land of green valleys, rushing rivers, towering mountains. There was wild game and plenty of rich farmland.

Then one day, Papa sold their house. He and Mama packed their dishes and books and clothes and tools into wooden barrels and the Morgan family joined a wagon train heading west.

The trip took almost six months. It was uncomfortable and dangerous. Bess remembered the day their wagon was swept downstream when the wagon train crossed a raging river. Another day, a little boy fell beneath the wagon wheels and was crushed to death. Others got sick along the way and couldn't go on.

That was only last year, but to Bess it seemed a long time ago. Now Papa had gone back to Missouri with Marcus Whitman to bring more settlers to Oregon.

Bess hurried down the path, looking for their cow. She found Sybil standing quietly beside her stall, swishing her tail. Bess rubbed the cow's velvety nose. "Sorry to keep you waiting, old girl," she said.

She took the milking stool from the stall and sat down. Then she put the metal pail beneath the cow's udder and

squeezed. The milk made a pinging sound
when it hit the empty bucket. When it was
full, Bess put a fresh bucket of oats in the
cow's stall and hung the stool on its peg.
"Bye, Sybil," she murmured. "See you tomorrow."

She stopped in the garden to pick
some strawberries to go with the flapjacks
Mama had promised. When she reached
the cabin, it was dark. No light showed
from inside. She hurried up the steps and
left the milk and berries on the table.
"Mama?"

"Bess? Is that you?"

"Mama, what is it?"

"Light the lantern, honey. The
matches are in the cupboard."

Bess fumbled in the gloom for the tin
box of matches. She struck one and
turned up the wick on the lantern. A weak
circle of light bloomed in the darkness.

Holding the lamp high, Bess made her way to the feather bed.

Mama lay beneath the covers, her teeth chattering despite the summer heat. Her skin felt cold and damp, and her eyes glittered. "I've got a fever, Bess. A bad one."

"What should I do, Mama?"

"Wet a cloth and wash my face. Then make some tea."

Bess scurried about the dim cabin, following Mama's orders. When the teapot was empty, Bess sat beside the bed, dipping the cloth in cool water and washing her mother's face.

"Will you be all right, Mama?" Bess asked.

Mama managed a weak smile. "By tomorrow I'll be good as new, and fussing at you about your quilt. You'll see."

All night Bess sat beside Mama's bed, listening to the tick, tick, tick of the clock on the mantel and the gentle soughing of the wind in the trees. She was too worried to sleep.

Where was Papa, just when she needed him most? And what if Mama was still sick in the morning? What would she do then?

Chapter Two

Mama was no better when morning came. Bess bathed her mother's face with cold water and made more tea, but Mama was too weak to sit up. And still, Papa was not home.

As soon as it grew light, Bess saddled her horse and set out on the road for Salem. Dr. Winslow had taken care of Papa last summer. Surely he would know what to do for Mama now.

Before Bess had gone half the distance to town, the rain came. She dug her heels into the horse's sides and urged him on through the storm. Ahead of her, black clouds boiled up and jagged lightning split the sky. The horse veered off the road and stood wild-eyed and trembling beneath the trees.

"Come on, Sam," Bess coaxed, jerking on the reins. "Come on, boy. Let's go, Sam."

At last, Sam found the road again and they went on. When they got to Salem, Bess tied the horse outside the doctor's office. A little bell above the door tinkled when she opened it. The sharp smells of camphor and iodine filled her nose. The rain beat steadily on the tin roof. Bess shivered in her wet clothes.

"Hello!" she called. "Anyone here?"

No one answered. Bess looked around. The walls of the doctor's office were covered with pictures cut from magazines. There were pictures of lakes and mountains, pictures of locomotives, pictures of young men in a boxing ring and young women at a Sunday picnic. On the doctor's shelves were jars of castor oil and calomel, bottles of pills and strange-looking herbs, tins of strong-smelling ointments, boxes of yellow soap. In the corner was a microscope and a box of glass slides.

The door opened and Dr. Winslow came in, rain dripping from his black hat. "Well, it's Bess Morgan, isn't it? Your pa back yet?"

"No, sir, and Mama's sick. She has a fever. A bad one," Bess said. "You have to come, quick."

The doctor looked out at the driving rain. "Not much of a day for traveling.

But then, sick folks can't help the weather, can they?"

"No, sir. Will my mother be all right?"

He shook his head. "Can't tell you that till I know what's wrong with her, girl. But I can tell you this, I'll do my best."

He put some medicines into his bag and handed Bess a blanket. "You'll ride in the buggy with me, and we'll tie your horse on behind. No sense getting any wetter than you are already."

They went out to the doctor's buggy, and Bess climbed inside. It smelled of leather and tobacco and wet wool. Bess tucked the blanket around her knees while Dr. Winslow tied Sam to the buggy. He handed her his bag and picked up the reins.

"*Yah!*" he yelled to his horse, and they started back through the rain to the cabin. On the way, Bess told him how Mama had fallen while they were dancing, and how she'd bathed her mother's face and made tea for her to drink.

"But this morning, she couldn't even sit up," Bess finished. "And she couldn't open her eyes."

"*Hmm,*" said the doctor.

"What do you think it is?" Bess asked.

"Sounds like a fever all right," Dr. Winslow said. "Well, we'll soon see."

Bess sprang from the buggy before Dr. Winslow drew up in the yard. She burst through the door of the cabin. "Mama? How are you?"

The cabin was dim and quiet; the only sounds were the ticking of the clock and Mama's shallow breathing. Bess lit the lantern and held it for the doctor when he came in.

He bent over the bed. "Mrs. Morgan? It's Dr. Winslow. Nod your head if you can hear me."

Bess watched her mother's head

18

move against the embroidered pillowcase.

"Good, that's good." He took out his stethoscope and listened to Mama's breathing. Then he lifted her eyelids and looked into her eyes, and felt her forehead.

Bess stood beside the bed, chewing on her bottom lip. At last the doctor spoke. "Looks to me like swamp fever. Saw a lot of it when I was in the army down south. Don't see too many cases this far north, though."

"Will she get better?" Bess asked.

"Eventually." He took a bottle from his bag and gave it to Bess. "This is quinine. Give it to her twice a day with plenty of tea and as much food as she can manage."

Bess sniffed the medicine. "It smells awful!"

"Indeed it does." Dr. Winslow smiled at her. "But it usually does the trick. She needs complete bed rest, Bess. And don't be scared if she gets better, then suddenly takes a turn for the worse. That's normal with swamp fever. Just keep giving her the medicine and in a few weeks she'll be good as new."

Tears of relief rolled down Bess's face. "Thank you, Dr. Winslow."

"You're quite welcome, my dear. Now, I should be on my way. I'll check with you in a few days, and in the meantime, I'll send Mrs. Fairchild along to give you a hand."

He patted Bess's shoulder. "Don't you worry about a thing. Everything will be all right."

Bess watched him run out to his buggy and disappear into the rain. She made some tea, and sliced the loaf of bread Mama had made the day before. She stirred the bitter-smelling medicine into the tea and helped her mother sit up and drink it. Then she went out to milk the cow and gather eggs.

By the time she got back to the cabin, the rain had stopped. Her mother slept peacefully in the feather bed.

Bess took off her shoes and her wet clothes and crawled into the warm bed next to Mama. When she woke again it was morning.

The medicine seemed to be working. Mama smiled at Bess and sat up, resting her back against the pillows. "What day is it?"

"Thursday," Bess said, frowning. "At least I think so."

"Poor darling. I'm sorry about this," Mama said. "Were you scared?" She smoothed Bess's bright gold hair.

"A little," Bess admitted. "I wish Papa were here."

Mama smiled. "Me too. He could bring both of us breakfast in bed."

"Are you hungry, Mama?" Bess slid from the bed and padded barefoot across the room. "I can make you some tea and scrambled eggs."

Mama turned pale. "Oh, no, I don't think I'm up to eating eggs just yet. How about some bread and butter?"

"All right," Bess said. "And you have to take more quinine, too."

"Quinine?" her mother said quietly. "Then whatever I've got is serious."

Bess nodded. "Dr. Winslow said it's swamp fever."

"Swamp fever? Is he sure? I thought only people in the tropics got that."

Bess filled the teapot and lit the stove. "That's true, mostly. But he says he's seen a few cases here."

Her mother watched while Bess sliced the bread and opened a jar of strawberry jam. "You're so grown up, Bess. Sometimes it's hard for me to remember you're only ten."

Bess grinned. "Sometimes it's hard for *me* to remember I'm only ten. Here."

She gave her mother a plate and poured the tea. When they had finished, she bathed her mother's face and straightened the bed covers. "There now. You go back to sleep. I've got chores to do."

Mama's eyelids grew heavy. "What would I do without you, Bess?"

Bess took her bonnet from its peg and went out to the garden. Yesterday's rain had left it too muddy to do much hoeing, but she weeded the rows of summer squash and picked an apron full of beans for supper. Maybe Mama would like some bean soup. She left the beans on the porch and went to milk the cow. While the fresh milk cooled, she hauled water from the river and pulled the last of the onions from the onion patch. One of the young pear trees had fallen over in the storm, and Bess tied it to a stake with a strip of cloth from her sewing basket.

She went to the henhouse to gather eggs. The sun rose higher, and the wind rustled the branches of the fir trees, making shifting patterns of light and dark on the ground. In the distance came the *clop-clop-clop* of horses' hooves on the road. Bess lifted her head and listened, and caught a glimpse of a gray horse and black buggy coming through the trees.

Chapter Three

She went out to the gate. Mrs. Fairchild had come, just as the doctor had promised. Mrs. Fairchild reined in her horse and waved to Bess. "Come and help me, child."

Bess left her egg basket and went to Mrs. Fairchild. The woman peered at her from behind her thick glasses. "How's your ma? Doc Winslow says she's got the swamp fever."

"She seems better today," Bess said. "But I'm glad to see you. It's scary out here all alone without Papa."

Mrs. Fairchild shook her head, and both her chins quivered. "Pish and tosh, girl," she said. "When I was no older than you, I raised three brothers all by myself back in the Dakotas. Fought off the Indians more than once, I tell you. Now, if you want to be good and scared, try fighting Indians, that's what I say. Here, take these pickles."

Bess took the pickles and the warm pie tin Mrs. Fairchild handed down. The smell of freshly baked apples and cinnamon made her mouth water.

"Watch it now, here I come," Mrs. Fairchild said, and she put one brown boot out of the buggy and jumped down. The buggy squeaked when she landed. Mrs.

Fairchild straightened her blue bonnet
and adjusted her white starched apron.
She took a wicker basket from the buggy
and said, "Let's go see your ma."

They went in. Mama opened her eyes
and smiled when she saw their visitor.
"Martha. How kind of you to come."

Mrs. Fairchild waved her pudgy fingers. "It was nothing, Sarah. I can't stay
long now. Mr. Fairchild is feeling kind of
poorly himself and I promised I'd watch
the store this afternoon. I don't think he
got a moment's sleep last night."

"I'm sorry to hear that," Mama said.
"Bess, make some tea for Mrs. Fairchild,
would you?"

"Land's sakes, don't go to no trouble
for me," Mrs. Fairchild said. "I expect this
child has been running around like a
headless chicken these past few days."

She patted Bess on the head. "I can
make the tea. Why don't you sit for a spell?

Looks to me like you've been working all morning."

Bess sat on the wooden chair beside Mama's bed. It seemed strange to have another woman bustling about their cabin, but it felt good, too. It was hard to be ten and in charge of everything.

While she worked, Mrs. Fairchild told Bess and Mama about everything that was happening in Salem. A new minister was coming to start another church. The general store had just received some pretty new dress material all the way from San Francisco. And everyone in town was getting ready for the big fair to be held in just three weeks.

"It's terribly exciting," Mrs. Fairchild said. She took Mama's best tea cups from the cupboard and poured their tea. "There'll be a food fair, with everyone bringing their best pies and cakes. Mr.

Fairchild is in charge of sack races for the children and the ice cream social on Saturday night. Oh, and there's to be a quilting contest."

"What's that?" Bess asked.

"The ladies will bring their best quilts to be judged. There'll be cash prizes for the best ones. Last year, the best quilt brought two hundred dollars!"

Mrs. Fairchild nibbled on a tea cake from her basket. "I am so excited about my quilt," she said. "It's called Friendship and it has a huge pineapple in the center, stitched with real gold thread."

Mama set her tea cup on its saucer. "It sounds lovely, Martha. I wish I could see it."

"Well, I'd bring it out to you, but I'm not quite finished with it yet," Mrs. Fairchild said. "Everyone who has seen it says it's sure to take first prize."

"I'm sure they're right," Mama said.

"Will you be entering a quilt, Sarah?" Mrs. Fairchild asked.

"Not this year," Mama said. "I've been teaching Bess to quilt. Maybe next year."

"Really, Bess?" said Mrs. Fairchild. "You're making a quilt?"

Bess nodded. "It's not very good."

"Well, let's see it!" Mrs. Fairchild said. "Surely it's not as bad as all that."

Bess glanced at Mama, hoping not to have to bring out her quilt with its lumpy stitches and plain pattern. But Mama smiled and nodded, and Bess brought the quilt from its shelf in the cupboard.

"It's not very good," she said again, dropping the quilt onto Mrs. Fairchild's ample lap. "My stitches get all tangled up."

"Try using shorter lengths of thread," Mrs. Fairchild advised. She held up the quilt. "This isn't too bad," she said. "It's the Log Cabin pattern, isn't it?"

Mama nodded. "Log Cabin was the first pattern I learned to make when I was Bess's age. I thought it would be a good one to learn on."

Mrs. Fairchild folded the quilt. "It's coming along," she said to Bess. "In a few years, who knows? You might take first prize at the fair."

Bess doubted that, but she said, "thank you" and put the quilt away.

Mama said, "Bess, did you bring in the eggs this morning?"

"Oh!" Bess clapped a hand over her mouth. "I left them at the henhouse when Mrs. Fairchild came."

"Perhaps you'd go get them. We'll send some home with our guest."

"Oh, that's not necessary," Mrs. Fairchild said.

But Mama said, "Run along. And while you're out there, see if there are any strawberries left. I expect Mr. Fairchild will feel much better after eating some fresh strawberry shortcake."

Mrs. Fairchild laughed. "Land's sakes, you'll spoil him beyond all toleration, Sarah. But I admit, the idea of strawberry shortcake does make a body's mouth water."

"Go on then, Bess," Mama said. "I'm getting too tired to sit up much longer anyway."

Mrs. Fairchild nodded. "Soon as you're back, Bess, I'll be going. I brought you a ham, apple pie, a loaf of bread, and pickles. That should help you out for a few days."

"We're grateful to you, Martha," Mama said.

"You'd do the same for me," Mrs. Fairchild said. "Run on now, Bess. Your ma's tired, and I should be getting back."

Bess took a basket for the berries and went to the strawberry patch. When her basket was full, she gathered a few flowers for Mrs. Fairchild and went to the hen-house to get the eggs. That was when she heard Mrs. Fairchild's voice coming through the open window of the cabin.

". . . didn't want to say anything in front of Bess," Mrs. Fairchild said, her voice low. "But you've got to face facts, Sarah. He's been gone more than a month longer than he should have. Looks to me like he's not coming back."

"Joe wouldn't leave us here alone," Mama said. "He adores Bess. He would never abandon her. No matter what."

Bess froze. *They were talking about Papa!*

"All I'm saying is, you should think about what you're going to do if he doesn't come back," Mrs. Fairchild said. "How will you manage the orchards, the animals, the gardens, by yourself? Especially now that you're sick?"

"I have Bess," Mama said. "We'll manage if we have to. But Joe will be back, as soon as he can. You'll see."

"I hope you're right, Sarah. But you've made that trip. You know how dangerous it is. Joe could be killed by Indians or starved to death in the desert. For all we know, the whole lot of them could be drowned in the Snake River."

Bess couldn't listen anymore. She dropped her baskets of eggs and berries and ran for the riverbank as fast as she could. She threw herself on the soft moss and cried as if her heart would break. Papa dead? Impossible. He was the bravest and smartest man ever to travel the Oregon Trail. He would come back! He had to! Hot tears seeped from her eyes and wet the front of her dress. Why, oh why hadn't they stayed in Missouri?

After a long time, she went back to the house. Mrs. Fairchild's horse and

34

buggy were gone. Bess gathered up the eggs and berries and went inside. Mama was waiting for her.

"What happened, Bess? Mrs. Fairchild waited and waited for you." She eyed the damp hem of Bess's dress. "Were you playing beside the river again?"

Bess's bottom lip trembled and a single tear rolled down her cheek. "Has Papa left us here for good? Is he dead?"

"Is Papa . . . Come here, honey." Mama opened her arms and Bess fell into them sobbing. Mama rocked her back and forth.

"So you overheard Mrs. Fairchild talking about him, did you?"

Bess nodded. Mama's cotton gown felt smooth against her cheek.

"You know it's not polite to eavesdrop, don't you?"

"I didn't mean to," Bess said, sniffing. "Is it true, Mama, what she said?"

"Of course not. The wagon train has been delayed for some reason, that's all. Remember when we got snowed in halfway through the Blue Mountains?"

Bess nodded.

"We had to wait nearly a week before we could move on," Mama reminded her. "I'll bet that's where Papa is. Snug as a bug in a rug, waiting for the weather to clear."

"You really think so?"

"Yes, I do," Mama said. "And you mustn't worry anymore about it."

Bess swallowed hard. She wanted to believe that Mama was right. But . . .

"Mama, suppose Papa *doesn't* come back? What then?"

But Mama had fallen into a deep sleep, crumpled against the pillows like Bess's old rag doll.

Chapter Four

When morning came, Mama seemed
worse again. Her forehead felt hot and
she shivered beneath the covers. Bess
brought fresh water from the river and
bathed her mother's face. She made tea
and stirred the quinine into it. Mama

drank it and lay back against the pillows, her eyes dull with fever.

"Mama, can you eat something?" Bess coaxed. "Some bread and jam, maybe?"

"Not just now, honey. Let me sleep for a while." Mama's cold fingers closed around Bess's small ones. "Don't be scared. I'll be all right. You go look after Sybil and feed the chickens."

Bess took her bonnet from its peg on the wall and went out to do her chores. From his perch in the treetops, a yellow-feathered meadowlark sang her a greeting, and the river tumbled noisily over its mossy rocks. Bess checked on the fruit trees, milked Sybil and gathered eggs, wishing there was something she could do to make Mama feel better. Her gaze fell on the patch of summer flowers nodding in the breeze. Maybe a bouquet would cheer Mama up.

Bess had started cutting the bright

red zinnias and yellow marigolds when a horse and rider came down the road and stopped at the gate.

Bess stood up, her flower basket in her hands, and studied the man from beneath the brim of her bonnet. He was tall, taller than Papa, with dark hair and a dark moustache. He wore a black suit, a stiff white shirt, and a tie with stripes that reminded Bess of a Christmas candy cane.

He got off his horse and came up to the gate. "Morning, miss. Is your ma home?"

"My mother is very sick. She's got the swamp fever."

"Swamp fever?" The man's bushy eyebrows moved like two fuzzy caterpillars. "That's a good one! Nobody gets swamp fever in these parts. What are you trying to pull here, missy? Did that no-account pa of yours put you up to this?"

Bess's mouth dropped. "Papa isn't

here. I don't know what you're talking about. What do you want?"

He brushed the dust from his sleeves and glared at her. "I'll tell you what I want. I want the hundred dollars your pa owes me, and I want it now."

"A hundred . . ."

"That's right, missy. He signed a note, all nice and legal. But what am I doing talking to a child about such things? Where's your ma? Swamp fever, my eye."

He yanked open the gate and strode toward the cabin. Bess ran at his heels, calling, "Mister! Wait! Please don't wake up Mama."

But he knocked once on the cabin door and went in. Then he stopped in his tracks when he saw Mama asleep in the bed.

Bess stared at him, blinded by tears, her heart full of rage. How dare he barge in here like this!

He turned to her. "Well, so she *is* sick. But I still can't believe it's the swamp fever."

"Bess? Who's there?" Mama sat up and pushed her tangled hair away from her face. Then she saw the intruder and drew her covers up to her chin. "Who are you? What do you want?"

The stranger took off his hat. "The name is Trask, ma'am. Nathan Trask. And I'm awful sorry you're sick."

"Well, Mr. Trask, as you can plainly see, I'm in no condition to entertain guests," Mama said.

"This isn't a social call, ma'am. I've got business with your husband."

"He's away at the moment. With Mr. Whitman, as everyone around here knows."

"Yes ma'am. The truth is, your husband took out a loan before he left, and he signed a note to pay it back by the first of August. Now that's more than a month ago, Mrs. Morgan, and I just can't wait any longer. I need that money."

Mama reached for her water glass and took a long drink. "I'm sure you do, Mr. Trask. And if I had it, I'd gladly pay it. We all thought the wagon train would be back long before now. I'm sure my husband will make good on his promise the minute he gets back."

Trask shook his head. "Not good enough. I'm a lender, Mrs. Morgan. That's how I make my living. If I don't collect when the loans come due, I'm out of business."

Mama's cheeks were flushed. "Well, Mr. Trask, it seems we're at an impasse. You want money that I don't have. What would you have me do?"

He reached in his pocket for a paper. "Sign your farm over to me. You've got quite a little spread here. Nice orchard started, a good garden. I figure it's worth a hundred dollars and then some."

Mama's eyes glittered. "Sign the farm over to you? Have you lost your mind?"

"No ma'am. I'm just bound to have what's mine." He bent down to show her the fine writing on the paper. "The law says I have to give you thirty days' notice. If the debt isn't paid by then, I can take the farm, whether you sign the papers or not."

"Get off my land, Mr. Trask," Mama said. "Before I come out of this bed and throw you off."

"Very well. But I'll be back. And when I come, I'll be bringing the marshal with me. Then we'll see who's throwing who off this farm. Good day, ma'am. Missy."

Bess stood trembling beside the bed, listening to the man's heavy boots on the wooden porch. When he had gone, she kicked off her shoes and got into bed with

Mama. Tears seeped from Mama's closed eyes, and Bess wound both arms around her mother's neck.

"Don't worry, Mama. Papa will be back in time. I just know he will."

Mama nodded weakly and fell asleep, exhausted. Bess lay awake, watching dust motes dance in the shaft of sunlight coming through the window. Why hadn't Papa come back? Was he lost somewhere in the Blue Mountains? Had he been attacked by Indians, or trampled by a horse?

Thirty days, that man Trask had said. What would she and Mama do if Papa weren't back by then? Where would they live if that awful man took their farm?

Suddenly, Bess sat bolt upright in the feather bed. The quilt! Hadn't Mrs. Fairchild said there'd be a prize for the best quilt at the fair? If she could win the money, she could pay Mr. Trask and hold on to the farm until Papa got home!

44

Bess got out of bed and took her quilt from the cupboard. She spread it carefully on the floor and counted the squares still to be done. Five, six, seven, eight. She sighed. The fair was less than three weeks away.

Mama moaned softly and turned over in her sleep. Bess took down her basket and threaded her needle. This time, she would have to work patiently, as Mama had taught her. But how could she possibly go slowly when she had so little time?

For the rest of the day, Bess snipped lengths of blue and red and yellow and brown cloth and stitched them together on the Log Cabin quilt. The needle pricked her fingers, and her eyes burned from working the tiny stitches hour after hour, but she worked on.

When it grew dark, she lit the lantern and worked some more. Still, Mama lay in a fevered sleep. The clock on the mantel ticked into the silence. From the woods came the lonely hoot of an owl and the singing of crickets.

To keep from being scared, Bess hummed all the songs Papa had taught her. First she hummed "Turkey in the Straw," then "Sweet Betsy from Pike" and "Soapsuds Over the Fence."

Finally, when she could not hum another note or sew another stitch, she slept.

When she woke in the morning, Mama was sitting up in the bed, brushing her hair. Bess yawned and Mama smiled.

"Good morning, sleepyhead," Mama said. "I'm glad you're finally awake. You'll have to go into town today. We're nearly out of flour and salt, and the bread Mrs. Fairchild brought is gone."

"All right." Bess didn't tell Mama about the log cabin quilt. If she couldn't finish it in time for the fair, Mama would be even more discouraged. She would keep her plan a secret until the very last minute.

Bess changed her dress and brushed her hair. She picked up her bonnet and the last few coins Papa had left them before he went to join Mr. Whitman's wagon train.

"If you see Mrs. Fairchild at the store, you be sure and apologize to her for not coming back with her eggs and berries the other day," Mama said. "And not a word to her about what you overheard. Understand?"

"Yes, Mama." Bess bent over and kissed her mother's cheek. "Do you need anything before I go?"

"I'll be fine," Mama said. "But come home as fast as you can. I don't want you on the road alone after dark."

Bess saddled her horse and set out

for Salem. The sun shone, but she could smell autumn in the cool morning air. Soon, September would turn to October and then snow would blanket the valley. If Papa wasn't home by then, chances were he wouldn't come till spring. Bess urged Sam toward town. When they crossed the creek, she heard a sound like the crackling of wood underfoot. She stopped and turned to look around.

The woods lay in deep shadow. Birds flitted through the fir trees and squirrels raced among the branches, preparing for winter. Bess saw movement in the distance. She held her breath and strained her eyes, but now the woods were still. Had she imagined it, or had someone, or something, been following her?

She kicked the horse into a canter, and rode him hard the rest of the way. By the time she reached Mr. Fairchild's store,

48

her heart thudded against her ribs and her mouth felt dry.

"Well, Bess Morgan," said Mr. Fairchild from behind the counter. "You look as if you've been running from the devil himself."

"I thought I saw something—a shadow—in the woods," Bess said, panting.

"Well, I wouldn't worry about it. It was probably just the light playing tricks on you." Mr. Fairchild handed her a glass of lemonade. "Here. This'll make you feel good as new."

"Thank you." Bess drank the lemonade. It tasted cool and tart on her tongue.

She took the coins from her pocket. "Mama needs flour. And salt."

Mr. Fairchild put a bag of each on the counter, but waved away her money. "You keep that till your pa gets back. You might need it for an emergency."

"But Mama said . . ."

"Never mind that. You tell her I said for her to keep it. There'll be plenty of time to settle up once your pa is home."

"Hiram?" Mrs. Fairchild called from the back of the store. "Who's that you're talking to out there?"

"It's Bess Morgan," Mr. Fairchild said.

Mrs. Fairchild lumbered to the front counter, her chins quivering like a turkey's wattle. Bess felt her face turn hot. Could Mrs. Fairchild tell by looking at her that she'd listened in on the conversation with Mama?

"How are you, Bess?" Mrs. Fairchild said. "How's your ma?"

"Some days are better than others," Bess said. "She seems stronger today."

"That's a relief," Mrs. Fairchild said. "You're taking such good care of her, she'll be up and around again in no time."

Bess took a deep breath. "Mrs. Fairchild, I'm sorry I didn't come back with your eggs and berries the other day."

"Oh pish and tosh," Mrs. Fairchild said. "Don't worry your head for a minute about that, child. Me and Mr. Fairchild here eat more than we should anyway."

She poked her fat stomach. "Don't look to me as if I've missed too many meals."

Bess grinned. "I'm glad you're not mad at me. I have something important to ask you."

"Well, what is it, child?" Mrs. Fairchild peered through her glasses at Bess. "Speak up."

"I want to enter my quilt for judging at the fair," Bess said.

"Oh?" Mrs. Fairchild's white eyebrows went up. "But you've hardly begun, Bess. It takes a long time to finish a quilt. And besides, you're just a beginner. I'm afraid you wouldn't stand a chance against the others who are entering."

"But I *have* to win, Mrs. Fairchild!" Bess cried. "I *will* finish in time, even if I have to work day and night."

"My, my. Well, if you're *that* determined, I suppose I can't stop you," Mrs. Fairchild said.

She took a piece of paper from beneath the counter. "This is the entry form. Fill it out and bring it with you when you bring your quilt in. Take your quilt over to the Methodist church on the day before the contest, and someone will be there to help you hang it up. You can pay your entry fee then."

"Entry fee?" Bess asked.

Mrs. Fairchild nodded. "Twenty-five dollars. That's where we get the prize money."

Twenty-five dollars! Bess stared at the

paper in her hand. She and Mama were down to their last few coins. The entry fee might as well be twenty-five thousand dollars! Now there was no way she could win the money and pay off Mr. Trask. If Papa weren't home in thirty days, she and Mama would be thrown off their own farm.

"Bess? What's the matter?" Mr. Fairchild asked kindly.

"It's . . . nothing." Bess tucked the entry form into her pocket and picked up the sacks of flour and salt. "Thank you, Mr. Fairchild. I'll see that Papa pays you soon as he's home."

"You're welcome as the flowers in springtime, Bess," he said. "Now don't you be scared going home. There's nothing in the woods to hurt you, you hear?"

Bess nodded. She put the sacks in her saddlebags, unhitched Sam, and headed for home. She didn't worry about strange sounds in the forest or scary shadows hiding in the trees. She was too busy thinking about one thing: How she could possibly get twenty-five dollars to enter the quilting contest.

Chapter Five

Bess sat at the table, an open book in front of her. Mama had written out a set of arithmetic problems for her to work, and a long list of sentences to copy. But Bess's mind wasn't on her lessons. She was still thinking about the quilting contest.

Mama lay against her pillows, brushing out her hair and humming softly. The door to the cabin stood open and a cool breeze blew through the room.

Mama said, "Where's your mind, Bess?"

Bess looked up. "Hmmm?"

Her mother smiled. "I've been watching you. You haven't written a single thing in the last ten minutes."

"Oh. I've been thinking," Bess said.

"Thinking, or worrying?" Mama put her silver-handled hairbrush on the chair beside her bed.

Bess chewed on her bottom lip. "Worrying, I guess."

"Well, it won't make Papa get here one minute sooner," Mama declared. "So you might as well not worry."

"But what about that Mr. Trask?" Bess asked. "Will he really bring the marshal to throw us off our own farm?"

Mama sighed. "I don't know, honey. As soon as I get stronger, I'm going into town to see that lawyer your father met last year. He'll know what's to be done. Although Lord only knows where I'll get the money to pay him."

Bess slammed her book shut. "Money! Why, a person can't even breathe around here without it costing money. And lots of it, too!" She burst into tears.

"Why, Bess! What's got into you?" Mama asked.

Then Bess told Mama about her plan to win the quilting contest and pay off Mr. Trask. She took the entry form from her pocket and spread it on the bed. "See? It costs twenty-five whole dollars just to enter the contest."

Mama smoothed Bess's bright hair. "What a lovely girl you are, to want to help out. But Bess, you've barely begun your quilt. You can't possibly finish it in time."

"I can if you'll help me," Bess suggested.

Mama shook her head. "It wouldn't be fair. If you're to enter the contest, you must do all the work yourself."

Bess shrugged. "It doesn't matter anyway. Where am I going to get twenty-five dollars?"

Mama was quiet for so long that Bess thought she'd fallen asleep again. But finally, she said to Bess, "Do you really think you could win?"

"Mrs. Fairchild doesn't think so," Bess said. "She said a beginner wouldn't have a chance against all the grown-ups."

"I suppose she has a point there," Mama said, her face thoughtful. "Still, it may be our only chance to pay our debt to Mr. Trask."

She sat up straighter in the bed. "Go bring me my Bible."

Bess stood on a stool and took the

Bible from the shelf. It smelled dusty, and the leather cover crackled in her hands. She handed it to her mother.

Mama turned the thin pages, making a tiny rustling sound in the quiet room. At last she stopped. "Here we are."

Bess looked down. Three brand new ten-dollar bank notes lay between the pages. Thirty dollars! Where had that money come from?

Mama held the bank notes out to Bess. "Papa put this away for your schooling," she said. "And we vowed never to spend it, no matter what. But it seems we are in something of an emergency, you and I. I don't think Papa will mind if we borrow it for a while."

"Mama! Are you sure?" Bess still could not believe her eyes.

Mama nodded. "If you finish your quilt in time to enter the contest, you may use this money for the entry fee." She

59

grinned. "Of course, I'll expect you to pay it back out of your winnings."

Bess felt as if her heart had wings. She *would* finish the log cabin quilt. And she would do her best to win. When Papa came home, he would be proud to see what she had done. Bess put the money back in its hiding place and took her quilt from the cupboard. She could hardly wait to get started.

"Aren't you forgetting something?" Mama asked.

Bess clapped her hand over her mouth. "Sybil! That poor cow! She's probably bursting by now."

Mama laughed. "Go put the poor thing out of her misery and then you may work on your quilt."

Bess grabbed her milking pail and set off for the pasture. Cotton candy clouds mushroomed against the bright autumn sky, and the meadowlarks sang in the trees. Bess hurried along the path, humming to herself.

"Hooo-wee, hooo-wee."

Bess stood still, listening. What was that?

"Hooo-wee," came the sound again.

The forest went suddenly silent. The meadowlarks hushed their singing, the squirrels went still. In his pasture, Sam pawed the ground and pricked his ears.

Shadows moved silently along the river. And this time, Bess knew her eyes were not playing tricks on her. Three Indian men stole toward her, their footsteps whispering on the mossy riverbank.

Bess dropped her pail and ran for the cabin, her arms churning, her bare feet pounding the hard earth. Her heart felt too big for her chest. She opened her mouth to scream, but no sound came out.

She looked behind her. The three men loomed closer. Now Bess could see their dark faces, and the red and black markings on their arms and chests. They moved steadily, their eyes straight ahead, so close now that Bess could hear their breathing.

"Mama!" At last a scream tore from her throat. She kicked open the cabin door and fell into her mother's arms.

"Indians!" she yelled. "Coming up the river."

Mama's hands fluttered. "Oh, dear Lord. Bess, are you sure?"

"I'm positive, Mama. I saw them. Three men. Wearing war paint."

"Bar the door," Mama directed. "Then help me push the cupboard in front of it."

Mama threw back the covers and stood up, wobbling on her frail legs. Her white nightdress flapped about her feet as she helped Bess move the furniture in front of the door.

"Go get Papa's gun," she said. "And then hide under the bed, Bess. And don't come out, no matter what happens. Do you hear me?"

"Yes, Mama," Bess said. "I'm scared."

"Me, too. Hurry now."

Bess brought Papa's rifle and then scooted on her stomach beneath the bed. She lifted the edge of the quilt and looked out. All she could see were the wooden legs of the cupboard and the table, and Mama's bare feet moving back and forth across the floor.

Then Bess heard footsteps on the wooden porch, and the terrifying cries of the Indians. They pounded the door, rattling the hinges, their screams breaking the afternoon stillness.

"Mama!" Bess cried. "I'm scared!"

"*Shhh!* Be still now, and . . ."

Bess heard a clatter, then a thud. She lifted the quilt a little higher. "Oh!"

Mama had fainted! She lay in a white heap on the floor, the rifle beside her.

The pounding at the door grew louder, and the Indians' cries more terrifying. Then, with a loud crack, the door gave way, the cupboard toppled, and a huge pair of brown moccasins stole across the sunlit floor. Bess bit her lip to keep from screaming. The Indian was headed straight for her mother!

Bess's heart hammered in her chest. Her teeth chattered and her knees shook. But she had to help Mama. She rolled from beneath the bed and grabbed Papa's rifle. Too scared to take aim, she crouched beside the bed, held the rifle to her shoulder and fired.

The rifle kicked against her shoulder. The Indian let out a yelp of surprise and jerked backward toward the door. Bess held her breath, her fingers trembling against the cold trigger. Her ears hurt with the effort of listening.

The Indians' cries grew faint, then stopped. Cautiously, Bess stood up and looked around. The cupboard drawers stood open, and the cabin door swung crazily on its bent hinges, its latch splintered.

Mama moaned softly and opened her eyes. "What happened?"

"You fainted," Bess said.

Mama sat up. "The Indians! Bess, are you all right?"

"I think so."

Then Mama spied the rifle, still draped across Bess's arm, and the splintered door latch.

"Did you shoot them?" she asked, her eyes wide.

"I missed. Scared them, though."

"Thank goodness."

Mama leaned against the bed and

closed her eyes, her face damp with sweat, her arms still trembling.

"Do you think they'll come back, Mama?" Bess asked.

"I don't know, honey. It may have been nothing more than a hunting party, but we'll have to be more careful for a while."

"How will I milk Sybil? And what about Sam? What if the Indians try to steal him?"

Mama thought for a moment. "We'll bring Sybil and Sam up from the pasture and tie them out by the gate. Not even the Cayuse are brave enough to steal livestock from our front yard."

"What about the chickens?"

"There's nothing we can do about them," Mama said. "If the Indians are hungry, maybe they'll take the chickens and leave everything else alone."

66

She pulled her nightdress over her head. "Bring my blue dress, and find my shoes."

"But, Mama, you're too sick to walk so far. You should go back to bed."

"I'll be all right. I can't let you go down there alone. Hurry Bess, let's get Sam and Sybil up here before dark."

Bess helped her mother dress. They righted the cupboard and looked out. Mama reloaded the rifle. "Let's go," she said, her voice low. "Quickly, now."

Bess followed her mother past the cabin and down the path to the pasture. They found the cow standing beneath a tree. She bawled when she saw Bess. At the far end of the pasture, the horse stood watching them.

"You go get Sam," Mama said quietly. "I'll bring Sybil."

Bess ran to her horse and grabbed a

handful of his dark mane. "Come on, Sam," she whispered. "Let's go, boy."

Sam lumbered along beside her, and soon they caught up with Mama and the cow. Mama put her fingers to her lips and they started up the path. When they reached the front gate, they tied the horse and the cow to the porch posts. Mama stood watch with the rifle while Bess milked the cow and fetched pails of water, oats, and hay.

They went inside, and Mama lowered herself onto the bed. Beads of sweat stood on her lip and her damp brown curls clung to her forehead. "Help me, Bess. I think I overdid it."

Bess helped her mother lie down, and drew up the covers. She brought a glass of water and sponged Mama's face with a cool cloth.

"Better, Mama?"

"Yes, much better." Mama smiled up at her. "What a brave girl you are."

Bess swept aside her books and papers and took out her log cabin quilt. She spread it on the table, and the cheerful pattern unfolded in the dim room like a flower opening in the desert.

"Remember now, take your time and make neat stitches," Mama murmured.

Bess picked up her needle. For a long time there was no sound except the ticking of the clock and the snip, snip of her scissors. When it grew dark, she lit the lamp and the flame made dancing shadows against the cabin walls.

"Bess," Mama said at last. "You should stop for a while. You'll ruin your eyes."

"Just a little longer," Bess begged. "I'm almost finished with this row."

Outside, Sam whinnied and Mama stiffened. "What was that?"

Bess went to the window and parted the red-checked curtain. She peered into the darkness, her heart racing. Had the Indians come back? All she could see were Sam's shiny eyes, and the gleam of the metal bell around the cow's neck. "I don't see anything," she reported. "It was probably just the wind."

"Probably." Mama gave her a tired smile. "I guess I'm a little jumpy tonight."

"Why don't we sing?" Bess suggested.

And they did. Mama sang "Hay in the Meadow" and "Missouri Skies" and Bess sang "Sweet Betsy from Pike." Then they sang some hymns, and when they had sung all the songs they knew, they started all over again.

At last Mama's eyelids grew heavy, and Bess brought more tea and quinine. Mama fell asleep, one hand on her chest, the other resting on the butt of Papa's rifle.

Bess picked up her needle again. All night long, she sat in the dim lantern light, listening for sounds of trouble in the darkness and stitching, stitching, stitching on her Log Cabin quilt.

Chapter Six

As the day for the fair drew near, Bess rarely left her quilting, except to care for Mama and the animals. The Indians had not returned, but Mama decided to keep Sybil and Sam tied at the front gate, just in case. Each morning, Bess stepped off the porch, milked the cow, fed the horse, and

D. Anne Love

gathered eggs from the henhouse. She fried the eggs and made biscuits for breakfast, then unrolled her log cabin quilt and set to work.

Mama seemed stronger. She spent part of each day sitting in her chair by the window, watching the squirrels and birds chasing through the fir trees, and reading aloud from one of the books the Morgans brought from Missouri.

At last, Thursday came. Tomorrow, Bess would take her quilt to the church, along with her twenty-five-dollar entry fee. And on Saturday, everyone from miles around would come to Salem for the fair.

"Will you come to the fair with me, Mama?" Bess asked, without looking up from her stitching. Her silver needle made a tiny ticking sound against her thimble.

Mama looked up from her book. "I'd

love to, but I'm afraid the trip is a bit too much for me just yet."

Bess nodded, disappointment showing on her face. She had hoped Mama would be there to see her win the quilting prize. And she *would* win! She had to! Otherwise, there would be no farm left for Papa to come back to.

Mama put her finger in her book to mark her place. "Next year, we'll all go to the fair," she promised. "You, Papa, and me. Why, we might even stay overnight at the hotel. Wouldn't that be fun?"

Bess nodded. She'd never been inside the hotel, but once, on a trip to Salem with Papa, she'd glimpsed its red-carpeted staircase and glittering chandelier. It seemed very grand. But a year was a long time away. First she had to finish the quilt.

Her fingers flew across the fabric, making row after row of tiny stitches. A breeze ruffled her hair and rustled the pages of Mama's book. A meadowlark sang. Sunlight slanted through the window and made a gash of light across the cabin floor. Bess worked on. She hardly noticed when Mama left her chair to light the lantern.

"Time for supper, Bess."

Bess looked up. Darkness had fallen. An owl called from the treetops. Mama set their plates on the table.

"I'm not hungry," Bess said. Suddenly, her shoulders ached, and her eyes burned. She let the quilt drop to the floor.

"Poor child. You've worn yourself out," Mama said. She gathered the quilt and spread it on the bed. "Come on now. Eat something, Bess, and rest your eyes. What good will it do if we're both too sick to work?"

Bess stood up and her feet tingled. She sat at the table and ate the bread and butter Mama gave her.

Mama said, "You've done a fine job on the quilt, Bess. Even if you don't win, you should be very proud of yourself. Papa will be proud, too. No matter what."

Bess hugged her mother and picked up her needle once more. Click, click, click went the needle against the thimble. The mantel clock chimed the hour. Eight. Nine. Ten.

"There!" Bess said at last. "Finished!"

Mama looked up. A wide grin split her face. "Bess! You did it! You really did it!"

Mama got out of bed and helped Bess fold the Log Cabin quilt. She wrapped it in clean muslin to protect it from dust on the ride to Salem. Then she got the Bible from the shelf and took out the three bank notes. "We'll pin the money inside your dress so it doesn't get lost," she said.

But Bess didn't hear her. She had fallen fast asleep, face down on the table.

The sun hung just above the treetops when Mama shook Bess awake on Friday morning. Bess rubbed her eyes. They felt scratchy and too big for her face. Mama brought a cool wet cloth. "Here. Wash your face, and you'll feel better," she said.

Mama made flapjacks for breakfast, and helped Bess pack a lunch for the trip to Salem. Then they packed Bess's best blue calico dress and her best bonnet to wear to the fair the following day. Mama had arranged for Bess to stay overnight with the Winslows.

"Now you be sure and mind your manners," Mama reminded Bess.

Bess threw her brown leather saddle over Sam's back and tightened the cinch. "I'll remember."

"And don't forget to thank Mrs. Winslow for letting you stay with her."

"Yes, Mama." She lifted the bridle over Sam's head.

"And be sure to get your five dollars in change when you pay your entry fee."

Bess looked up, hands on her hips, and grinned at her mother. "Anything else?"

Mama came down the steps, her white nightdress swirling about her ankles. She took Bess in her arms. "You're the finest, bravest human being I've ever known," she said against Bess's hair. "Just be careful and come back safely."

"I'll be all right," Bess said, trying not to think about the Indians who had invaded their cabin.

Bess swung into her saddle. Mama handed up her bundle of clothes, her lunch pail, and finally, the Log Cabin quilt. When everything was tied in place, Bess smiled down at her mother. "Take care of yourself, Mama. I'll be back soon."

"Good-bye!" Mama waved as Bess rode off toward town.

Salem buzzed with activity. Along Main Street, wooden bleachers had been set up. Tents sprang up in the vacant lot next to Mr. Fairchild's store, and the hotel manager put out the No Vacancy sign. At the far end of the street, three men were busy building a wooden platform for tomorrow's band concert. Horses stood tied to every pillar and post in town. Buggies, buckboards, and wagons lined the dusty street.

Bess rode Sam to the Methodist church, carefully untied her quilt and went inside. A woman with hair the color of ripe strawberries sat at a desk in the hallway.

Bess said, "I've come to enter my quilt in the contest."

BESS'S LOG CABIN QUILT

"Have you now?" the woman asked, surprised. "Aren't you a bit young for this, dear?"

"I'm almost eleven," Bess said. She unpinned the money from her bodice and handed it to the woman. "I'm Bess Morgan. Here's my entry fee."

The woman's mouth made a small O. She took Bess's three bank notes, gave her five gold pieces in change, and carefully wrote out a receipt. "Well, Bess Morgan," she said. "Take your quilt into the church parlor and the ladies will help you put it up."

Bess took her quilt into the church. Two gray-haired ladies bustled about, hanging quilts on heavy cords that stretched along all four walls. Such beautiful quilts! Bess's heart sank when she looked at the tiny stitches, the fancy designs of birds and flowers, hearts and stars in every color of the rainbow. Some of the quilts had satin borders, and patterns so intricate that it made Bess's head hurt just to look at them. How could her plain Log Cabin quilt compete against such beautiful designs? For a moment, she thought of turning around and going back home, but then she remembered the frightening look in Mr. Trask's eyes, and his warning to Mama. If they didn't pay Papa's loan, he would take the Morgans' farm.

"May I help you, dear?" one of the ladies asked.

"I'd like to enter my quilt," Bess said. She handed the woman her receipt.

"Right this way," the woman said. She helped Bess drape her quilt over the cord. When the quilt was hung, they stepped back to adjust it. The woman ran her fingers over Bess's tiny stitches. "This is fine work," she said.

"Thank you." Bess stood back, comparing her quilt to the others. Now she could see that she had indeed done a good job. Her quilt might not be as fancy as some, but the pattern was perfectly straight; the rows of red and yellow, brown and blue matched neatly at the corners. She felt a little better.

Bess wandered along the rows of quilts, studying them. Here was Mrs. Winslow's red and white quilt in the pattern Mama called Lone Star. Next to it was a pink and blue one called Turkey Tracks, and a yellow and white one called Hummingbird.

She came to a white quilt with a huge pineapple in the center. The pineapple was worked with such tiny stitches, in such rich colors, that it looked almost real. It was outlined with shiny golden threads that glittered in the sunlight. This must be Mrs. Fairchild's quilt. The one she told Bess and Mama about the day she came to visit. Bess leaned in for a closer look and ran her fingers over the shimmering stitches.

"Hey! You! Get away from that quilt!" said a voice behind her. Bess wheeled around. It was Mrs. Fairchild.

"Bess Morgan!" Mrs. Fairchild said, frowning. "What are you trying to do? Get dirty smudges all over my quilt?"

"No, Mrs. Fairchild! I—I was just admiring it. It's very beautiful."

With her gloved hand, Mrs. Fairchild brushed her quilt. "I worked for a solid year on this quilt, and now here you are getting it all filthy. And the day before the contest, too!"

Bess searched very hard, but she couldn't see even a speck of dirt on the quilt. "I'm sorry," she said. "I didn't mean any harm."

"Didn't you?" Mrs. Fairchild's eyebrows went up. Now she didn't seem anything like the kind woman who had visited

Mama just days ago. Her expression reminded Bess of the dark thunderclouds that boiled up over the valley in summer. "Even if you manage to ruin my quilt, yours still won't win, Bess," she said. "I told you. You're just a beginner. There are too many other quilts that are much more beautiful."

"But I *have* to win!" Bess said, trying very hard not to cry. "Mr. Trask came to see Mama. He said Papa owes him a hundred dollars and if we don't pay it, he's going to take our farm."

Suddenly, Mrs. Fairchild's features softened. She peered down at Bess. "Is that so?" she queried. Her voice seemed kinder now.

Bess nodded. "That's why I *have* to win, Mrs. Fairchild. It's our only chance."

Just then, Mrs. Winslow bustled into the church, the pink feathers on her hat

84

bobbing in the breeze. "Bess Morgan! There you are! I've been looking all over for you. Oh, hello, Martha," she said to Mrs. Fairchild.

"Hello, Elizabeth." Mrs. Fairchild gave her quilt another pat. "I really must be going. I'll see you later."

Mrs. Winslow knelt in front of Bess. "What's wrong, child? You look worried. Is your mother feeling worse?"

Bess shook her head. "Mrs. Fairchild scolded me. She thought I was trying to get her quilt dirty so mine would win. But I *wasn't*, Mrs. Winslow. Honest!"

"Well of course you weren't." Mrs. Winslow patted Bess's shoulder. "Never you mind about her. I hate to say it, but Martha Fairchild is a proud woman. Winning means everything to her. But her bark is much worse than her bite. Don't worry. She'll live."

Mrs. Winslow stood and took Bess's hand. "Come on now. It's almost suppertime. You must be exhausted."

With one last glance at her Log Cabin quilt, Bess followed Mrs. Winslow out of the church. They went over to where Sam stood dozing at the hitching rail. She took her bundle of clothes from the saddle.

"Don't worry about Sam," Mrs. Winslow said. "My husband will bring him along when he comes home for supper."

They walked along the wooden sidewalk past the blacksmith shop, the hotel, and Dr. Winslow's office. Mrs. Winslow stopped, cupped her hands to her eyes and peered through the dirt-filmed window.

"Hmmm. Just as I thought. Mrs. Carmody is in there again," she said. "That poor soul has more complaints than the rest of this town put together."

Mrs. Winslow shook her head and her

86

hat feathers bobbed again. "Come on, Bess. There's no telling when the doctor will be home."

"What's wrong with her?" Bess asked, as they walked up the hill to the Winslows' white clapboard house.

"Mostly, I think she's just lonely." Mrs. Winslow set her package on the porch and unlocked the door with a long brass key. "Her family all died of influenza the first winter they were here and she has nobody to talk to now. So she goes to Dr. Winslow complaining of aches and pains and Heaven knows what else. Here we are."

Mrs. Winslow held the door open and Bess went into a cool, dim hallway. A crystal chandelier sparkled overhead. Pictures of ladies on horseback hung on the wall. To one side sat a green velvet sofa and a table with a bouquet of flowers on top.

Mrs. Winslow took off her hat and set

it on the table. She smiled at Bess, her blue eyes kind. "Let me show you to your room."

They went up a curving staircase to a sunny room overlooking an orchard and a pond. The bed was covered with a white lace spread, and the wallpaper was yellow, with tiny sprigs of blue flowers on it. There was a mirror, a chest, and a table with a yellow pitcher and washbasin.

Mrs. Winslow unrolled Bess's bundle of clothes and shook out her blue calico dress. "Let's hang this up so it'll look nice for tomorrow," she said. "Why don't you wash up and have a nap. I'll call you when the doctor gets home."

"Thank you," Bess said. She untied her shoes and unpinned her hair. Mrs. Winslow closed the door.

Bess listened to the woman's steps on the carpeted stairs. She poured water into the basin and washed her face and hands.

Then she carefully folded back the lacy spread and lay down on the bed. She closed her eyes but thoughts circled in her head like horses on a merry-go-round.

What would happen if she didn't win the quilting prize? Would Mr. Trask really take their farm? And where was Papa? Was Mrs. Fairchild right? Had Papa simply gone away and left her and Mama to fend for themselves in Oregon?

Bess punched her pillow and turned over. No. Of course Papa hadn't left them. He would come home, as soon as he could. The question was, would she and Mama and the farm still be there when he did?

Chapter Seven

The next morning, Bess could barely remember Dr. Winslow's coming home and
the supper the three of them ate in the
Winslows' wood-paneled dining room.
When she got out of bed, the sun was up,
dappling the braided rug on the floor,

glinting off the mirror hanging above the washstand.

Hurriedly, Bess washed her face and hands and dressed in her blue calico dress. She took out her bonnet and went downstairs.

Dr. Winslow sat drinking coffee, his newspaper open on the table. "There you are, Bess. Did you sleep well?" he asked.

"Yes, thank you." Bess stood uncertainly in the doorway.

Dr. Winslow set his cup on its saucer and peered at her over the top of his paper. "Are you hungry?"

Mrs. Winslow bustled out of the kitchen, a plate of muffins in her hands. "What a question!" she said to her husband. "Of course she's hungry. Aren't you, Bess? Come on, sit down now. The fair opens in an hour and we don't want to miss a thing!"

Bess sat. The muffins, full of blueberries and cinnamon, smelled good. She ate two while the Winslows drank their coffee. At last, Dr. Winslow said, "I have to ride out to the Buckman place to check on Edward. I'll be back before noon."

"Be careful, dear," Mrs. Winslow said.

He nodded and picked up his black bag and his hat. "Good luck at the quilting contest," he said.

"Thank you," Bess and Mrs. Winslow said together. Then they both laughed.

"Oh, that's right," the doctor said. "I forgot you've entered the contest, too, Bess." He looked from one to the other of them, amused. "In that case, I hope you both win."

When he had gone, Bess went out to check on Sam. Dr. Winslow had unsaddled him and fed him a bucket of oats. He swished his tail and neighed softly when she rubbed his muzzle. Bess leaned her face against Sam's velvety one. "Wish us luck, boy," she whispered.

Mrs. Winslow came out in a green dress and a matching hat. "Ready, Bess?"

They walked into town along the dusty street crowded with people, buggies, wagons, and horses. Red, white, and blue flags fluttered in the breeze, and knots of people gathered on every corner.

Everyone seemed to be in a good mood. Men laughed and thumped each other on the shoulders, women chatted in the shade of the buildings, children chased each other, darting in and out among the wagons. On a grassy spot near the hotel, Mr. Fairchild was busy organizing the sack races. Bess watched as a dozen boys from neighboring farms and towns chose partners for the three-legged race, and hopped crazily toward the distant finish line. When it was over, Mr. Fairchild gave everyone a lollipop from his store.

"Come on, Bess," Mrs. Winslow said. "Let's go find a seat for the concert."

They found a shady spot beneath a tree and Mrs. Winslow spread a blanket. They sat down. Soon a man in a white hat came around, carrying glasses of lemonade. Mrs. Winslow bought them each a glass and they sipped it slowly while the band played. Bess leaned against the tree and closed her eyes. Music always made her think of Papa. How she missed the way he laughed, the way he played his harmonica, keeping time with the toe of his boot against the cabin floor.

A tear seeped out and Bess brushed it away. Just for today, she would try not to worry about Papa and Mama and the farm. Just for a little while, she would try to enjoy the fair.

The people gathered for the concert clapped and cheered. Two boys put their fingers in their mouths and made loud whistling sounds. The concert was over.

Mrs. Winslow stood up and folded their blanket. "Wasn't that lovely?" she asked, her cheeks flushed. "I do love those marches! So stirring!"

She put her hand on Bess's shoulder. "I promised to help judge the jams and jellies," she said. "Will you be all right for a while?"

"I'll be fine," Bess said.

Mrs. Winslow nodded. "I'll meet you at the church at eleven o'clock. We want good seats for the quilt judging."

Then Bess heard a loud squeal and turned around. A girl in fat red braids and a bright plaid dress ran up to her. "Bess? Bess Morgan? Is it really you?"

"Liza?" Bess could hardly believe her good luck. Liza McCormick had been her best friend on the long trip from Missouri to Oregon. But Liza's father had decided to go on to Walla Walla with the Whitmans. Bess had not seen her friend in a long time.

Bess explained to Mrs. Winslow that the Morgans and the McCormicks had traveled together on the Oregon Trail.

"This is splendid!" Mrs. Winslow said. "Now I won't feel so bad about leaving you alone for a while."

Liza looked up at Mrs. Winslow. "You have nothing to worry about," she declared. "I'm almost thirteen. I'll take good care of Bess."

Mrs. Winslow smiled. "Something tells me Bess Morgan can take care of herself, but I'm most grateful for your company, Liza." She picked up her bag. "You girls have a good time. Don't forget now, Bess. The church. Eleven sharp."

"I won't," Bess said.

Liza slipped her arm through Bess's. "Tell me everything that's happened since you got to Salem," she said. "Don't leave out a single thing."

The two girls made their way through the crowd, stopping now and then to watch a magician perform his tricks, or to listen to men making speeches in the park. Bess told Liza about their farm, about Papa's leaving to bring more settlers to Oregon, and about Mama's swamp fever.

Liza's eyes grew round when Bess told how she'd fired Papa's rifle to scare off the Indians, and she laughed when Bess talked about having school right in her own cabin because there was no real school nearby.

"No school! How lucky!" Liza said. "You can do your lessons any old time you want."

"Yes, but I miss having friends," Bess said.

"There are plenty of children at the

mission where I live," Liza said. "And it's safer from the Indians, too. My mother says she wouldn't dare live out in the valley all alone."

"When Papa gets back, we won't be alone," Bess said.

Liza studied her friend. "You're worried, Bess. I can tell."

Bess nodded. "Everyone says he should have been back a month ago."

Liza said, "I know. Everyone at the mission is anxious for news of Mr. Whitman, too."

"What do they say at the mission, Liza? Has there been any news at all?"

"Not a word," Liza said. "Or at least any that you can depend on. You know how people like to talk. Mostly it's just wild rumors."

"Like what?" Bess persisted.

Liza shrugged. "I don't know. Oh,

things like, someone found a bunch of burned out wagons and . . ."

"And what? Tell me."

Liza blew out a breath so strong it ruffled her coppery bangs. "And they said there were some scalps sticking on poles, but you know how people like to talk, Bess. It's probably not even true."

Scalps. Bess swallowed hard. What was it Mrs. Fairchild had said that day at the farm? That Papa might have been killed by Indians? She shook her head. She wouldn't think about it. She just wouldn't.

Liza squeezed Bess's hand so hard it hurt. "Don't let it bother you, Bess. I told you it's just rumors. Nobody knows anything for sure." She took a paper bag from her pocket. "Here. Have a lemon candy and let's go watch the magic show again."

After the show, the girls made their way to a booth in front of the hotel, where men from the church were passing out free lemonade. They each took a glass and sat in the shade, sipping it. When they finished, Bess said, "I have to meet Mrs. Winslow at the church. Come with me to watch the quilt judging."

"I can't, Bess," Liza said. "I have to meet my parents. My father is helping with the parade and I have to help Mother with the twins."

"Twins?" Bess asked, puzzled.

Liza laughed. "Oh, that's right! You don't know about them. I have two baby brothers now. Born last November."

"Oh, what fun!" Bess said. "Imagine having not one, but two sweet, cuddly children to play with."

Liza grimaced. "You wouldn't think it's so much fun if you had to wake up when they get sick in the night, or clean

them up when they make messes. Sometimes, they're a real pain."

"I don't care," Bess said. "I still think
it would be wonderful."

Liza hugged her friend. "I have to go
now."

"Write to me?" Bess asked.

"I promise," Liza said. "If you'll write
back."

"Oh, I will," Bess promised. "The
very next day."

Liza laughed. "Good-bye, Bess Morgan. Maybe I'll see you here next year."

"Bye!" Bess called. She watched until
Liza's red braids were lost in the crowd.
Then she went to the church.

It was already filled with ladies, mur-
muring and laughing together, walking
up and down the long rows of quilts. Bess
saw the judges, two older women wearing
yellow ribbons on their blouses. They each
had a pencil and a small notebook.

Please, Bess said silently. *Please. I have to win.*

She joined the long line of ladies admiring the quilts. She passed a blue and white quilt in a pattern called Stormy Seas and a pale yellow one called Wedding Ring.

When the line turned the corner, Bess gasped. The spot where Mrs. Fairchild's fabulous pineapple quilt had hung was empty! Bess craned her neck, trying to see where it had been moved. She scanned the rows of neatly hung quilts, but the pineapple quilt had disappeared.

Bess looked up just in time to see Mrs. Fairchild making her way into the church. She bustled down the aisle, and the other ladies moved aside to make room for her. In her dark gray dress and matching bonnet, she looked like a huge ship slicing through the water. And she was headed straight for Bess!

Bess's heart raced. Yesterday, Mrs. Fairchild had accused her of dirtying the pineapple quilt. Now the quilt was gone. Would Mrs. Fairchild think she had stolen it?

Bess glanced left and right. Where was Mrs. Winslow? *She* knew Bess was innocent.

Then Mrs. Fairchild stopped, right in front of Bess. "There you are, Bess Morgan!" she cried. "Where the devil have you been? I've been looking all over for you!"

Chapter Eight

Bess swallowed. "Mrs. Fairchild . . ."

"Come with me," Mrs. Fairchild said.
She took Bess's hand and led her out of
the crowded church. They sat on a stone
bench in the shade of a tree.

"Mrs. Fairchild," Bess said again. "I

don't know what happened to your quilt, I
swear it! I didn't take it, honest I didn't."

"Oh stop blathering, girl, and listen
to me." Mrs. Fairchild opened her bag and
took out her fan. "I know you didn't take
the quilt. I took it down myself. Last
night."

Bess's mouth dropped. "But *why?*
You were so mad at me for even touching
it. And you said yourself that it was sure to
win."

"I know what I said. And I'll admit, I
was madder than a hornet when I thought
you'd gotten it dirty."

Mrs. Fairchild's fan went back and
forth, stirring the heat. "I worked on that
thing all year, practically day and night,
and to tell you the truth, I'm awful proud
of it. But I thought about what you said,
about needing to win the prize money to
pay off that Trask man." She shook her
head, and her chins quivered. "He's a bad

one, all right. This town will be much better off when we get a real bank and don't have to depend on greedy men like him for loans."

Bess stared at Mrs. Fairchild, trying to make sense of it all.

Mrs. Fairchild went on. "So, I took my quilt out of the contest. To give your Log Cabin quilt a better chance."

From far away came the sound of band music and the beat of drums. The parade was about to begin. Bess said, "I don't know what to say."

Mrs. Fairchild patted her hand. "You don't have to say anything. Even with my quilt out of the running, you still have plenty of competition in there."

She stood up. "Let's go find Elizabeth. It's almost time for the judging to start."

They found Mrs. Winslow in the hallway, talking to the lady with the strawberry-colored hair. She smiled when she saw Bess.

"Did you have a good time with your friend?"

"Oh, yes!" Bess said. "Guess what? She has two baby brothers. Twins!"

"Merciful heavens!" Mrs. Fairchild said. "Two babies at once! Can you imagine?"

"Only just," Mrs. Winslow said. "Shall we go in?"

They took their seats and waited for the judges to begin. Bess felt like a wound-up spring. She twisted her handkerchief into a tight little ball and then unrolled it again. Her stomach felt funny, as if she'd swallowed a stone.

At last one of the judges stood up. "First place in the quilting contest goes to Rebecca Poole for her quilt called Lover's Knot."

Hot tears stung Bess's eyes, but she clapped as the winner came forward to claim her prize. "Congratulations, Rebecca," the judges said, and the ladies clapped again.

Everyone waited for the next winners to be named. Bess held her breath. The only sounds were the rustle of the ladies' dresses and the quiet clearing of throats.

The other judge stood up. "There's a tie for second place," she announced.

Bess gripped her damp, balled handkerchief and squeezed her eyes shut. This was it. Her last chance to claim a prize and save the farm.

"The first winner is Patience Howell for her quilt, Star of Bethlehem . . . and the second is Bess Morgan for her Log Cabin quilt."

Bess felt frozen to her chair. Had she heard right? Or was it only wishful thinking?

D. Anne Love

Mrs. Winslow laughed and hugged her. "Bess! Bess! You won! Go on up there!"

Everyone clapped and cheered. Patience Howell winked at Bess and kissed her cheek. "Congratulations!" she whispered. And then the judges handed each of them an envelope.

"Thank you," Patience said to the judges.

"Thank you," Bess echoed.

She floated back to her seat. Then she opened the heavy envelope. A handful of gold pieces glittered in the light. Quickly, Bess counted them. Twenty, forty, eighty . . . She stared up at Mrs. Fairchild in disbelief. A hundred dollars, exactly!

Mrs. Fairchild whispered, "Congratulations, Bess."

Bess threw her arms around Mrs. Fairchild. "Thank you! Thank you!"

BESS'S LOG CABIN QUILT

"Land's sakes, child, don't choke me to death!" Mrs. Fairchild said, disentangling herself. "You worked hard, Bess. You deserved to win."

"But you worked hard, too," Bess said. "And your quilt is beautiful. I'm sure it would have won."

Mrs. Fairchild's blue gaze met Bess's. She said quietly, "There are some things in life more important than winning."

The contest ended. Mrs. Winslow said, "You'd best let me hold onto that envelope for you, Bess."

She tucked it safely inside her drawstring bag. "Now then, I don't know about you, but I'm starved. And that husband of mine promised to be back in time for lunch."

They made their way out of the crowded church and onto the dusty street. The parade had ended. Bess scanned the faces in the crowd, hoping to see Liza again. But Liza had gone, and Bess followed Mrs. Winslow and Mrs. Fairchild back to the hotel.

"Well, I'd better check in at the store and give Hiram a hand," Mrs. Fairchild said. "It'll be busier than a beehive this time of day."

"Good-bye, Martha," Mrs. Winslow said. "Will we see you later for the ice cream social?"

Mrs. Fairchild nodded. "You will if these old feet of mine hold out. Good-bye, Bess. Take care of your mama now, you hear?"

"Yes, ma'am. And thank you, Mrs. Fairchild. For everything."

"Pish and tosh. I didn't do anything. You go on now and have a good time." She waved and turned down the street, her gray skirts making a trail in the dust.

"Well," said Mrs. Winslow. "I see my husband isn't back yet after all. Would you like to have lunch at the hotel?"

"I'm too excited to eat," Bess said. "I can't wait to get home and tell Mama the news. I won! I actually won!"

"Then we should celebrate!" Mrs. Winslow said. "Come on, Bess. You have to eat *something*."

They ate at a table covered with a white linen cloth and set with real silver and pale green china. Mrs. Winslow ordered a tray of tea sandwiches and tall glasses of iced tea with mint and lemon, and chocolate cookies for dessert.

After lunch, they found Dr. Winslow in his office, bandaging a young boy's foot.

"What happened?" Mrs. Winslow asked, her voice kind.

"Stepped on a piece of broken glass in the river," the doctor answered for his patient. He turned back to the boy. "I told you boys not to swim down there behind the saloon. People throw all kinds of things in the water back there."

The boy winced when the doctor tied off the bandage.

"There now, that should do it." Dr. Winslow took a tin of yellow salve from his shelf. "Put this on twice a day and keep that foot dry till it heals up, you hear me?"

"Yes, sir."

"And stay out of that river bottom."

"I will."

The boy left, jingling the bell over the door.

The doctor washed his hands and dried them on a white cloth. "Well now, who's for ice cream?"

"Bess and I want some," Mrs. Winslow said. "And then I think Bess will want to go home."

"So soon? Before the fireworks?"

"Bess tied for second place in the quilting contest," Mrs. Winslow said. "I think she's ready to go home and spread the good news."

"Well, Bess, congratulations!" the doctor said. "I expect your ma will be right proud of you."

"Yes sir," Bess said. "I expect so, too."

They went out to where the ice cream was being served. Bess had a dish of peppermint and a dish of strawberry. Then she was ready to go home.

Mr. Winslow brought the buggy and tied Sam on behind. Mrs. Winslow folded the Log Cabin quilt back into its muslin cover and handed Bess her clothes. She took Bess's envelope from her bag and pinned it to the bodice of Bess's blue calico dress.

When Bess was settled in the buggy beside the doctor, Mrs. Winslow leaned in and kissed her cheek. She smelled of violets and summer sunshine. "Congratulations, Bess. And good luck."

"Thank you, Mrs. Winslow. For everything."

"You're welcome, my dear. Come and visit me anytime."

Dr. Winslow said, "I won't be late, Elizabeth."

They started off down the road. The sun lay low against the horizon. Golden light filtered through the trees. The shadows grew longer, and the trees became dark shapes beside the road.

Bess felt suddenly tired, but too excited to sleep. Just wait till Mama found out about the hundred dollars! That awful Mr. Trask couldn't take their farm now, no matter how long it took Papa to get back home.

The buggy rumbled across the wooden bridge and rounded the last curve. Light from the cabin made a pinprick of gold in the purple-shadowed valley. When they drew closer, Bess could see that the door to the cabin stood wide open. And a strange horse stood at the front gate. Bess's heart raced. Was Mama all right? Who would be visiting the farm this time of night?

Then she heard the bright, reedy sounds of a harmonica and Mama's lilting laughter.

"Papa!" she yelled.

Dr. Winslow stopped the buggy in the yard and Bess scrambled out, shouting, "Papa! Papa!"

A shadow appeared in the doorway. "Bess? Is that you?"

"Papa!" Bess threw herself into his arms. He felt solid as a tree, and smelled wonderfully of soap and leather and pipe tobacco. He scooped her into his arms and twirled her around the porch.

D. Anne Love

"You're home, Papa! I knew you'd come back!" Bess cried.

Mama came to stand in the doorway. She wore a blue dress Bess had never seen before, and a matching ribbon in her hair.

Dr. Winslow held out Bess's clothes, and the Log Cabin quilt. "I believe these are yours," he said, an amused smile on his lips.

"Thank you!" Bess said. "Oh, I'm sorry, Dr. Winslow, I . . ."

"That's quite all right." He pumped Papa's hand and slapped him on the back. "We'd about given up on you, Joe."

"*I* hadn't!" Bess declared. "I knew you'd be back!"

"Oh you did, huh?" Papa smiled and ruffled her hair. "Well, I'm mighty glad to be back. For a while there, it looked like we might not make it."

117

"What happened, Joe?" Dr. Winslow asked.

"That's what I want to know, too," Bess said, still clinging to Papa's hand. "What took you so long?"

Papa cleared his throat and leaned against the porch railing. Mama winked at Bess. Her smile said, *Here comes one of Papa's stories.*

"Things started out well enough," Papa began. "We made good time for the first two weeks. Then the rains set in. You know what that does to the oxen."

Dr. Winslow puffed on his pipe and nodded. "Poor beasts kill themselves trying to haul wagons through a sea of mud."

"That's a fact," Papa said. "We brought everything to a halt and waited for the rains to stop."

"So *that's* where you were!" Bess said.

"Oh, that was just the beginning," Papa said. "The ground finally dried out

enough to move on, and we headed for the
South Platte. By then, several women and
children were sick, and we were in a hurry
to get to the doctor at Fort Laramie."

"What happened then, Papa?" Bess
asked.

"We made it to the river all right,"
Papa continued. "But the water was so
high, we couldn't cross. Meanwhile, more
and more people were getting sick. I left
Marcus with the wagon train and rode out
alone to bring the doctor back."

"That was foolish of you, Joe," Mama
said into the gathering dusk. But Bess
could hear the love and admiration in her
mother's voice.

Papa shrugged. "Maybe. But I
couldn't let them die. We lost too many as
it was."

Dr. Winslow sucked on his pipe, making a red glow in the darkness. "Traveling
that trail is a dangerous business, all right.

But you did the right thing, Joe. I'm proud of you, boy."

"You'd have done the same thing if you'd been there," Papa said. He took a deep breath. "Anyway, when the waters finally went down, we crossed the river, but by then, we'd lost a lot of time." He grinned at Mama. "Sorry to be so late for supper, Sarah."

Mama clasped Papa's hand. "You're home now. That's the important thing."

"Indeed," Dr. Winslow murmured. "Well, I should be getting on back. I promised Elizabeth I wouldn't stay late."

"Thank you for taking care of Bess at the fair," Mama said. "And for bringing her home."

"You're welcome," Dr. Winslow said. "I left Sam tied at the gate."

They watched him drive away. Then Bess said, "Come into the house. I have something to show you."

"What is it, Bess?" Papa asked.

"You'll see."

Bess made them sit at the table. The lantern light cast deep shadows on their faces but she could see anticipation in their eyes. She unpinned the envelope from her bodice and put it on the table.

"Open it, Mama."

Mama picked up the envelope and looked inside. She gasped. "Oh, my goodness, Joe. Look at this! There must be a fortune here!"

"One hundred dollars," Bess said proudly. "Exactly."

"One hundred . . ." A slow smile spread across Mama's face. "Bess! The Log Cabin quilt!"

"I tied for second," Bess said. "That horrible Trask man can't take the farm now."

Mama jumped up and hugged her, and Papa laughed and laughed. At last he said, "You don't have to worry about Nathan Trask, little one. I sent him a hundred-dollar bank note as soon as the wagon train got back to Fort Boise."

"Don't you see what this means, Bess?" Mama asked. "Now all this money belongs to you. For your schooling."

"Soon as Salem gets a proper bank, we'll open an account for you," Papa said. "We'll get your own passbook with your name right there on the cover." His hands made words in the air. "Miss Bess Morgan. How about that?"

Bess looked at him, her expression troubled.

"What is it, Bess?"

"It's Mrs. Fairchild," Bess said. Then she explained how Mrs. Fairchild had taken her own quilt out of the contest to give the Log Cabin quilt a better chance. "I'm not sure I ought to keep the money," she finished.

Papa hugged her. "Tell you what. Tomorrow, you and I will ride into Salem and straighten it out. All right?"

Bess nodded. Papa had a way of making everything turn out just right.

And then, he brought out his harmonica. He began to play, keeping time with his boot on the wooden floor. Mama laughed and clapped her hands. They sang until the lantern burned low, and they were still singing the next morning when the sun came up.